· Friends ·

by Catherine Peters

illustrated by Maria Diaz Strom

HEATH **D.C. Heath and Company**
Lexington, Massachusetts   Toronto, Ontario

We are best friends.

We like to read books.

We like to play games.

We like to make music.

We like to paint pictures.